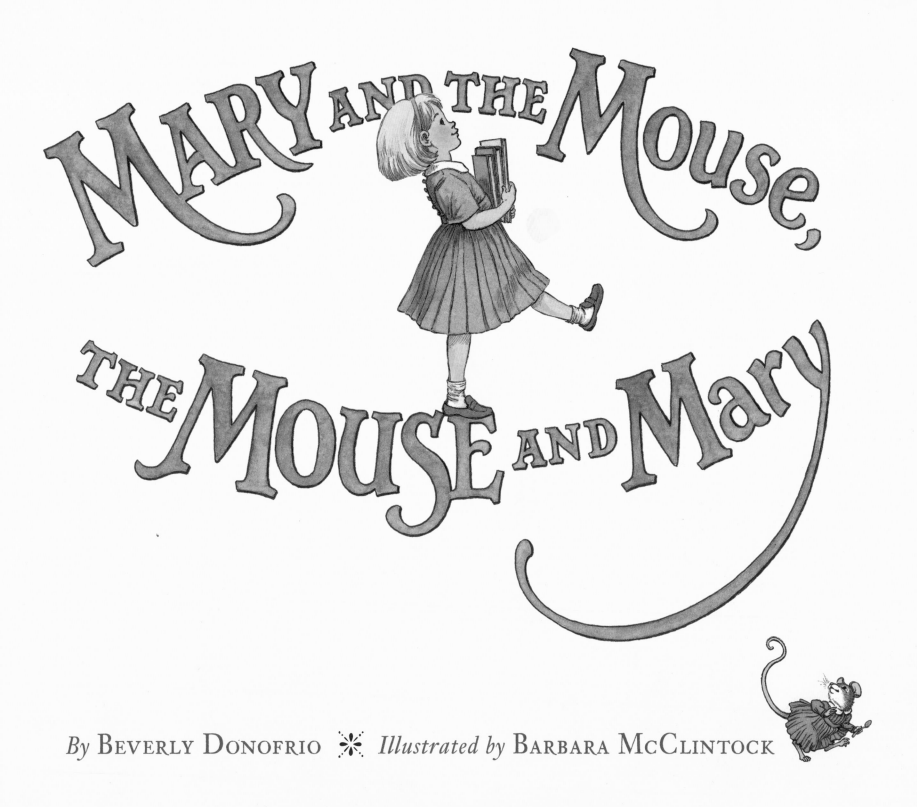

Mary and the Mouse, the Mouse and Mary

By Beverly Donofrio ✳ Illustrated by Barbara McClintock

schwartz & wade books · new york

Mary lived in a big house
with a very little mouse.

The Mouse lived in a little house
inside a very big house, with Mary.

Mary had a mother and a father and a sister and a brother.

The mouse had a mother and a father and a sister and a brother, too.

Every day Mary went to school down the street.

Every day the mouse went to school in the hollow of a tree.

Mary learned to draw

and read,

to count

and sing.

The mouse learned to do all the same things.

One night after dinner, Mary helped clear the table and dropped a fork.

The same night after dinner, the mouse helped clear the table and dropped a spoon.

Mary picked up the fork and noticed the mouse. The mouse picked up the spoon and noticed Mary.

Mary's parents had always warned her, "Stay away from mice. They have fleas and germs, and sometimes they'll bite."

The mouse's parents had always warned her, "Stay away from people. They're sneaky and mean and sometimes they'll lure you into traps."

So Mary didn't tell her family about the mouse.

And the mouse didn't tell about Mary.

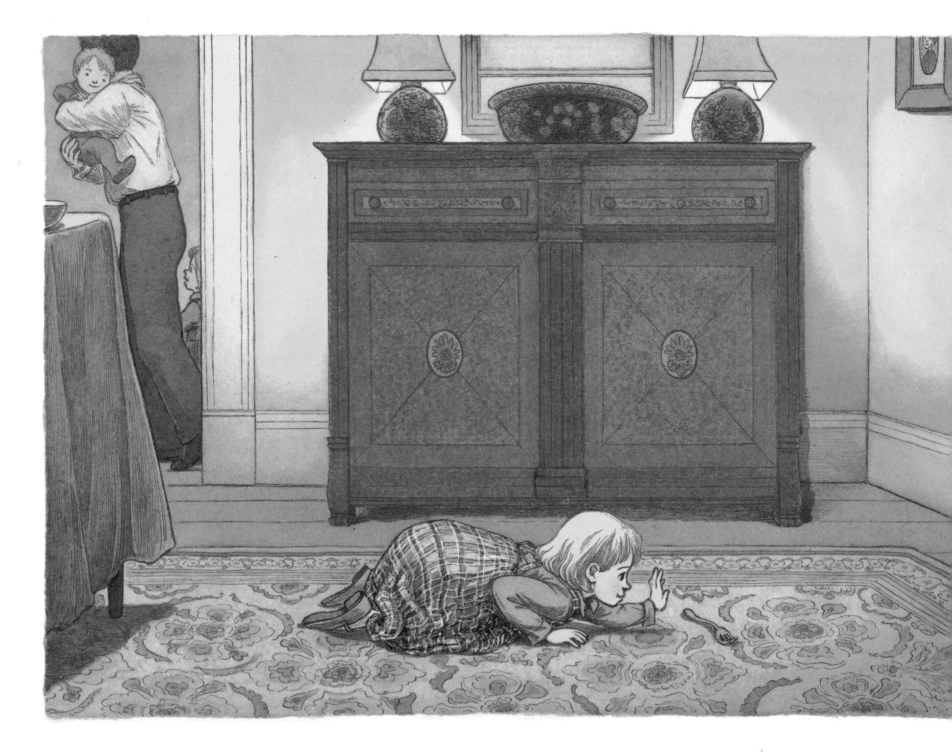

The next night after dinner, Mary accidentally on purpose
dropped her fork so she could wave at the mouse.

That same night after dinner, the mouse accidentally on purpose
dropped her spoon so she could wave at Mary.

Every night from then on, Mary dropped a fork
to wave at the mouse.

All those same nights, the mouse dropped a spoon
so she could wave at Mary.

But then Mary grew up and moved from the big house.

And the mouse grew up and moved from the little mouse house inside the very big house.

Mary missed the mouse.

The mouse missed Mary.

When Mary became a mother, she and her family lived in a very big house.

When the mouse became a mother, she and her family lived
in a little house inside a very big house, with . . . guess who?

Every day Mary's daughter, Maria, went to school around the block.

Every day the mouse's daughter, Mouse Mouse, went to school in the hollow of a rock.

Maria learned to draw

and read,

to count

and sing,

and to play baseball.

For lunch, Maria ate strawberry yogurt, grapes, and two cookies.

Mouse Mouse learned to draw

and read,

to count

and sing,

and to play hopscotch.

For lunch, Mouse Mouse ate Swiss cheese.

Then one night at bedtime, Maria dropped her book.
When she picked it up, she discovered the mouse house.

That same night at bedtime, Mouse Mouse dropped her book, too.
When she picked it up, she discovered Maria staring into her house.

Night after night,

Maria accidentally on purpose
dropped her book

and smiled at Mouse Mouse.

Night after night,

Mouse Mouse accidentally on purpose
dropped her book, too,

so she could smile at Maria.

Then one night, Maria did something brave.

She climbed out of bed,

tiptoed over to the mouse house,

and got down on her hands and knees . . .

. . . just as Mouse Mouse did something brave, too.

She climbed out of bed

and tiptoed out of the mouse house.

And at exactly the same moment,
Maria whispered loudly to Mouse Mouse,

and Mouse Mouse whispered loudly to Maria,

"GOOD

For my grandson, Zachary —B.D.

For David —B.M.

Text copyright © 2007 by Beverly Donofrio
Illustrations copyright © 2007 by Barbara McClintock

Published in the United States by Schwartz & Wade Books
an imprint of Random House Children's Books
a division of Random House, Inc., New York

Schwartz & Wade Books and colophon are trademarks of Random House, Inc.

www.randomhouse.com/kids
Educators and librarians, for a variety of teaching tools,
visit us at www.randomhouse.com/teachers

Library of Congress Cataloging-in-Publication Data

Donofrio, Beverly.
Mary and the mouse, the mouse and Mary / Beverly Donofrio ; illustrated by Barbara McClintock. — 1st ed.
p. cm.
Summary: While Mary, a girl whose family lives in a big house, is learning things at school,
a young mouse whose family lives in a small house within the big one is learning the same things
at her school, and when the two eventually meet they become friends.
ISBN 978-0-375-83609-1 (trade) ISBN 978-0-375-93609-8 (glb)
[1. Friendship—Fiction. 2. Human-animal relationships—Fiction. 3. Mice— Fiction.]
I. McClintock, Barbara, ill. II. Title.

PZ7.D72225Mar 2007
[E]—dc22
2006030980

The text of this book is set in Archetype.
The illustrations are rendered in pen-and-ink, watercolor, and gouache.
Book design by Rachael Cole

PRINTED IN CHINA

10 9 8 7 6 5 4 3 2 1

First Edition